MON BUSINESS

Contents

GW00792862

MONKEY HOMES

Vervet Monkeys

Monkeys come in all shapes, sizes, and colours. There are about 200 different kinds of monkeys, and they live in many of the world's forests and grasslands.

Capuchin Monkey

Spider Monkey

Patas Monkey

3

Most monkeys spend their entire lives in trees. Monkeys that live in trees are usually small. They have long arms and are good at climbing. They can leap from tree to tree, high above the ground.

Cotton-Top Tamarin

Proboscis Monkeys

Brown Spider Monkey

5

Other monkeys, such as baboons, live on the ground. They walk around on all four feet.

Most monkeys are active during the day. At night, most prefer to sleep in trees.

Baboon

Chimpanzee

Did You Know?
A chimpanzee is not
a monkey. It is an **ape**.
Apes and monkeys
are **primates**.

MONKEY BODIES

Monkeys' fingers and toes are long and strong. They help them grip branches as they climb. Monkeys use their fingers to hold food as they eat. Monkeys' feet look a lot like their hands, and their big toes are often just like thumbs.

Woolly Monkey

Capuchin Monkey

Did You Know?
Capuchin monkeys
sometimes use tools,
such as stones or
sticks, to open oysters
and nuts.

Most monkeys have long tails. Their tails help them balance. Some monkeys, such as spider monkeys and woolly monkeys, can use their tails to swing from tree to tree.

Old World Monkeys

Pigtailed Macaques

New World
Monkey

Woolly Monkey

Did You Know?
Monkeys from Asia and Africa
are called **Old World
monkeys**. They cannot use
their tails to grip. Monkeys
from Central and South
America are called **New
World monkeys**. Most of
these monkeys can use
their tails to grip.

11

Monkeys are intelligent animals. Their eyes face forward, and most have good eyesight. They can hear well, too.

Old World Monkey

Mandrill

Golden Lion Tamarin

Did You Know?

Old World monkeys have nostrils that point down and are set close together. New World monkeys have nostrils that are further apart and point out to the sides.

MONKEY MEALS

Monkeys spend a lot of time looking for food. Most monkeys eat almost anything: leaves, grass, fruit, nuts, birds, frogs, and other small animals. Some monkeys even eat crabs and shellfish.

Crab-Eating Macaque

Chinese Snub-Nosed
Monkey

15

Monkey Families

All monkeys live in groups. Some monkeys live in small family groups. Some monkeys live in large groups called **troops**. While resting, monkeys **groom** each other. Grooming is one way that monkeys care for each other. Grooming helps keep order in the group.

Bear Macaques

Bonnet Macaques

Monkey Babies

Baby monkeys cannot take care of themselves. They drink milk from their mothers. Newborn monkeys are strong enough to cling to their mother's fur. As they get older, they ride on their mother's back. Young monkeys love to play. The troop watches them carefully, as **predators** will eat baby monkeys.

Chacma Baboons

Golden Snub-Nosed Monkeys

MONKEY TALK

If you were to visit a rainforest, you would hear "monkey talk". Monkeys call to each other to keep in touch with their group. They also call to warn each other of intruders or predators. Monkeys communicate by making sounds, clapping their hands, and jumping up and down.

Java Macaques

Black Howler Monkey

Did You Know?

The call of a howler monkey can be heard for about five kilometres. It is one of the loudest calls in the animal kingdom.

GLOSSARY

ape – a large, tail-less, and highly intelligent animal that can walk in an almost upright position. Gorillas, chimpanzees, orang-utans, and gibbons are apes.

groom – to clean and make tidy in appearance

New World monkey – a monkey that comes from Central and South America. Most have grasping tails.

Old World monkey – a monkey without a grasping tail that comes from Asia and Africa

predator – an animal that hunts and eats other animals

primate – any member of an order of animals that includes humans, apes, and monkeys. Primates have large brains and flexible hands and feet.

troop – a group of monkeys

INDEX